The Sleeping Giant of Goll

A Magical World Awaits You
Read

THE SECRETS OF DROON

The Sleeping
Giant of Goll

by Tony Abbott

Illustrated by Tim Jessell

SCHOLASTIC INC.
New York Toronto London Auckland Sydney
Mexico City New Delhi Hong Kong Buenos Aires

Book design by Dawn Adelman

No part of this publication may be reproduced, stored in a retrieval system, or transmitted in any form or by any means, electronic, mechanical, photocopying, recording, or otherwise, without written permission of the publisher. For information regarding permission, write to Scholastic Inc., Attention: Permissions Department, 557 Broadway, New York, NY 10012.

ISBN-13: 978-0-590-10844-7
ISBN-10: 0-590-10844-1

35 34 33 32 31 30 29 28 27 26   8 9 10 11 12/0

Printed in the U.S.A.   40
First Scholastic printing, February 2000

To Robert Boyd
and Amanda Barrett,
who know that plain old life
is an adventure

Contents

The Sleeping
Giant of Goll

One

The Magic Staircase

Bing-bing-bing!

It was early Saturday morning.

Eric Hinkle bounced up from his bed and shut off the alarm. He stared into the dim light, trying to recall his dream. Then he remembered it.

"Oh, no," he groaned. "Another night without dreaming of Droon!"

Dreaming was important.

After Eric and his friends visited Droon,

Princess Keeah told them that their dreams would tell them when to return. But it had been two weeks since anyone had dreamed of Droon.

That meant something was wrong.

Very wrong.

"The magic has to keep working," Eric said to himself. "It just has to!"

He dressed quickly and snuck down to the kitchen. He tiptoed to the back door and unlocked it. His best friend, Neal Kroger, slid in quietly.

"What's to eat?" Neal asked.

Eric stared at him. "Never mind food," he said. "What did you dream about last night?"

Neal took a deep breath. "The usual. Pizza."

Eric moaned. "Pizza? No wonder you're hungry."

"In my dream I was sitting in the middle of a humongous pizza," Neal said. "And I had to eat my way out to the crust. What about you?"

Eric sighed. "I was hitting a metal garbage can with a broomstick. Bing, bang, bong all night."

"Did it wake your parents?" Neal asked.

Eric gave him a look. "No. Then I woke up and realized it was just my alarm going off."

Neal shook his head as they tramped down the stairs to the basement. "Doesn't sound like we'll be going to Droon today," he said.

"I can't believe this," Eric groaned.

He remembered the first time he, Neal, and Julie discovered the magic entrance to Droon.

They were cleaning up Eric's messy basement when they found a small closet hidden under the stairs.

They went inside, flicked off the light, and — *whoosh!* — the floor turned into a rainbow-colored staircase.

Of course they went down the stairs.

Soon, they met Princess Keeah and the wizard Galen. They helped them fight a wicked and very powerful sorcerer named Lord Sparr. They had gone on lots of adventures since then.

Until now.

"What about the soccer ball?" Neal asked.

Princess Keeah had put a spell on their soccer ball. It would float in the air and become a globe of Droon when she needed them most.

Eric shook his head. "It's busted. Look."

He picked up the ball from its place on

the workbench. He dropped the ball to the floor.

Boing! It bounced back.

"This ball is only good for playing soccer."

Neal twisted his face into a frown. "Keeah said we'd return to Droon as long as the magic keeps working. I guess we're not going back."

"Oh, man!" Eric whined. "Julie will be sad."

"Or mad," Neal said. "We'd better tell her."

"Tell me what?" Julie said as she ran down the stairs. "Your mom said it was okay to come down, Eric. Am I too early?"

"More like too late," Eric said, shooting a look at Neal. "You didn't happen to have a dream about Droon last night, did you?"

Julie shook her head. "No . . ."

"That's it," Neal said. "Good-bye, Droon."

Julie grinned. "I mean, no, it wasn't just *any* dream. . . ." She headed straight for the door under the stairs.

"What?" Eric turned to her. "You mean —"

Julie laughed. "Last night I had the *ultimate* dream about Droon! I was floating high over the countryside. Then I saw a bunch of crowns — gold crowns — just sitting on a hilltop in the middle of nowhere!"

"Cool!" Neal exclaimed.

"But," Julie continued, "the coolest part was that I had a crown, too. I was Princess Julie! It was so awesome. We are definitely going back. Now!"

"Yes — yes — yes!" Eric yelled. "Let's do it!"

Julie quickly pulled open the small door. She waved her hand in. "Enter."

They all piled in. Neal closed the door. Julie flicked off the light.

Click! It was dark for an instant. Then —

Whoosh! The floor vanished beneath them. In its place was the top step of the magical rainbow-colored staircase. The staircase to Droon.

Eric jumped. "It's so good to be going back!"

"What can I say?" Julie said. "I'm special."

"You better believe it!" Neal said. "We'd actually have to finish cleaning Eric's basement if it wasn't for you!"

The three friends climbed down the rainbow steps. Cool air wafted up from below. It smelled sweet. The sky was pink and purple with streaks of bright orange. The sun was just about to rise.

"It's nearly dawn here," said Neal. "Hey, look at those trees."

The stairs ended in a misty grove of low, blossoming trees overlooking a clear green lake. The pink morning mist clung to the branches.

The kids jumped off the staircase just as the steps faded from sight. Eric knew the stairs would reappear when it was time to leave.

"I am so glad to be here," he said.

Julie looked around. "This is weird. Nine trees in a perfect circle. Trees don't normally grow in a circle. I think someone planted them this way."

"Maybe there are people nearby," Eric added.

Suddenly, the branches twitched.

"Did you see that?" Neal asked.

Before Eric could answer, the trees leaned their trunks toward the children.

Their rough branches thrust down like arms, grabbed Julie, and tightly curled their waxy leaves around her like fingers.

Then one of the trees pulled her off the ground.

"Helpppp!" she cried, struggling to get free.

But Eric and Neal couldn't help her.

One tree seized Neal by the ankles and pulled him up sharply. Another clutched Eric's waist and dragged him off his feet.

"Let us go, you overgrown twigs!" Eric shouted, smacking at the branches to get free.

But the trees only tightened their grip.

Two

The Land of Living Trees

"Now I know what they mean by plant food," Neal groaned as the tree holding him swung around. "And I think we're it!"

Julie's tree shook her up and down. "I promise I'll never eat a vegetable again. Just let us go!"

But the trees didn't let go.

They swung the kids high over the ground.

"Oo-oo-oo-oh!" Eric moaned. "I feel si-i-ick!"

The branches only coiled more tightly around him. He felt his strength slipping away.

"This can't happen!" he cried, gasping for breath.

"This is Droo-oo-oon," Neal cried. "Anything can happen!"

"I wish Keeah and Galen were here," Julie yelped. "They'd make these trees act like trees!"

At that moment, the sun began to rise.

Golden light slanted across the tree-tops.

Suddenly, the trees lowered their branches. They loosened their grip, and the children slid to the ground.

The trees coiled back to their original shapes.

And went completely still.

It was a quiet circle of trees once more.

Eric scrambled over to his friends. "Are you guys okay?" he asked.

"Ask me later," Neal coughed. "For now, let's just get out of here."

"I agree," Julie said, rubbing her arms where the branches had clutched her. "That sure was a Droonian moment."

Eric pointed to the lake at the bottom of the hill. "Let's get down there. Fast!"

They hurried to the sandy shore. The lake water glistened like glass. A light breeze rose off the surface.

"Peaceful," Julie said. "I wonder where —"

Splish! Splorsh!

The center of the lake began to bubble.

Neal stepped back. "Okay, now what?"

The water splashed. A small round eye pierced the surface. Then a long curved neck.

"Now — we hide!" Eric said, pulling Neal and Julie facedown in the sand.

"Sppp — ah!" Neal spit out sand as he looked across the water. "Terrific. Weird eyeball, long neck. This means only one thing. Sea serpent!"

"It's a lake," said Julie.

"Lake serpent!" Neal cried.

Soon, a body rose from the water. It was green and short and stubby, about the size of a small car. Sunlight flashed off its wet side.

"That's not a serpent," Julie said. "It's a . . ."

Vrrrm! It rumbled up onto the beach on fat green wheels. It lurched to a halt in the sand.

"A lake serpent with *wheels*?" Eric said.

Boing! A hatch on the side popped open.

A head appeared. Then a face. The head had bright orange hair that stood

straight up. In the middle of the face was a little pug nose.

"Max!" Julie exclaimed, jumping up and running over to the green machine.

Eric nudged Neal. "You were so afraid. Can't you tell the difference between a serpent and a submarine?"

"Afraid?" Neal shrugged. "I call it being *careful*."

Max clambered down from the hatch. He saluted with three of his eight legs. "Your favorite spider troll — at your service!"

He tapped the side of the sub. *Boink! Boink!*

Two more heads appeared from the hatch.

One was a young girl with long blonde hair. She was wearing a jeweled crown. The other was an old man with a long white beard and frizzy hair.

"Princess Keeah! And Galen!" Eric said. "Boy, are we glad to see you guys!"

"As we are to see you," Princess Keeah said. "You've come just in time to help us again."

"But we almost didn't make it," Neal said. "Some trees attacked us!"

"Then the sun rose and they let us go," Eric added.

"But mostly, I had the greatest dream," Julie said. "I even had a crown!" Then she told them all about it.

"Time will tell what it all means," Keeah said.

Galen smiled. "And what do you think of my latest invention? I call it my Below-Water-Motor-Powered-Transportation Vehicle."

Neal frowned. "You mean . . . a sub?"

"Sub?" Galen looked quizzically at

Neal. "I like that name. Sub. It certainly saves time."

"Which is good," Max chirped. "Because our time is running out. We're on a mission to find Lord Sparr!"

"Come aboard," Galen told the children. "I will explain."

A moment later, the three friends joined Keeah, Max, and Galen inside the small ship.

"Very cool!" Eric said as they took seats in a small round cabin. A control panel circled the front wall under a large window.

Max took hold of the controls. He pushed a large green button. Motors whirred behind them. The small ship rumbled down the beach to the water.

"We're on our way to Panjibarrh," Keeah said. "It's where the terrible giant, Zor, is supposed to have been buried. Lord Sparr is there."

"Dive, Max!" Galen commanded. "Dive!"

As the submarine splashed down into the green lake, Eric turned to his friends. "I think this is one adventure we'll always remember."

"For starters, we've never been attacked by trees before," Julie whispered.

"And I've never been in a sub before," said Neal. "Blub-blub!"

Three

Mirror, Mirror, in the Sub

The underwater world was beautiful. Thick bunches of sea vines coiled up from below. Bright red balloon plants puffed and unpuffed as they passed.

A school of yellow lumpy fish swam by, grinning right into the window.

"This is awesome," Eric said.

"I'm sure glad we're in here," Neal added.

Keeah smiled. "It won't be long now. Lord Sparr is nearby. We are getting close."

Galen pointed to a map on the control panel next to Max. "We have tracked Sparr to the Dust Hills of Panjibarrh. Legend says that is where the giant, Zor, lies buried in his lost tomb."

Eric shuddered as he remembered their last adventure. The evil sorcerer Sparr stole an ancient piece of jewelry. It was called the amulet of Zor.

The amulet was supposed to have the power to bring the giant back to life.

Max twittered nervously. "They say when the giant lived, he was taller than a mountain!"

"With luck, we'll stop the big guy," Neal said.

"With luck and with help," Keeah said,

touching a single white feather that hung on a silver chain around her neck.

The kids knew what it was.

It was a feather from Keeah's mother, Queen Relna. A spell had transformed her into a white falcon. But she had changed shape again.

No one knew what shape the queen had now.

The princess smiled, touching the feather again. "This makes me feel as if she is with me."

Zzzzt!

"What's that sound? Are we leaking?" Neal said, whirling on his seat. "Because I don't like leaks when I'm in a sub."

"It is Galen's magic mirror," said Max. "It has something for us to see. . . ."

The wizard stepped over to an old mirror hanging on the back wall of the sub.

The mirror allowed the wizard to see what was happening in different parts of Droon. The rippling surface flickered with a dull glow.

The kids already knew what was about to happen. They had seen the mirror before in Galen's tower.

Galen waved his hand and the mirror cleared.

"There's a dark room," Keeah said, peering at the image. "It's dusty and dirty and very large. Big stones are everywhere."

"It is a tomb," Galen said softly. "And look!"

Stomping toward the mirror was the sorcerer himself. Lord Sparr.

His long black cloak swept across the floor of the tomb. And the pointed purple fins behind his ears certainly didn't make him look any friendlier.

"I see we're tuned to the wicked sorcerer station," Neal said. "Man, he gives me the creeps."

Surrounding Sparr was a troop of plump, red-faced warriors in black armor. They carried shovels and picks and torches.

"Here!" the sorcerer said, pointing down.

Flickering torchlight glowed on a large, dusty stone. A strange symbol was carved on it.

"The sign of Zor!" Keeah gasped. "Sparr has already found the lost tomb!"

Sparr's eyes flashed. He shivered as he stood over the large stone. "So . . . I have found the lost empire. And the legend is true. Zor lies here."

"Lost empire?" Eric whispered.

Galen sighed deeply. "Droon is a world with a long past, my friends. Lord Sparr has discovered what remains of the ancient dark realm of Goll. It is an empire whose cities now lie buried beneath the earth but that once ruled this world. Goll is a lost civilization. An empire that time forgot."

"Too bad Sparr remembered," said Neal.

The sorcerer snapped his fingers, and his Ninn warriors began quickly digging around the edges of the stone.

Clank! Clong! Before long, the Ninns pulled the stone from the floor. They looked down. They backed away from the hole, trembling.

"Have you found . . . him?" Sparr said.

The Ninns muttered to themselves.

Sparr pushed them out of the way and leaned over the hole. His fins turned pale, almost white.

The mirror zoomed in. There, lying open to the flickering torchlight, was a large dark object.

"Oh, my!" Max muttered.

"What is it?" Eric asked.

"It's a . . . a . . . head!" Keeah gasped.

The head was six feet long from chin to brow. The large eyes were closed. The dust of centuries covered the cheeks and lips.

But the strangest part was the skin.

It was dark and smooth and glimmered golden red in the torchlight.

"He's . . . made of metal!" Eric said.

"Bronze," Galen muttered. "Zor is a giant made of bronze. He walked the earth long ago."

Neal stared at the mirror. "A giant, huh? If that's just his head, this guy must be huge!"

"Bigger than huge," said Eric. "Enormous."

"Enormous? Ha!" said Neal. "He's hu-mongous! He's colossal! He's —"

"Will you shhh!" Julie hissed.

"We are afraid, Lord Sparr," one of the Ninns whispered. "We want to go home."

"Home!" Sparr snarled. "My true home lies above, in the Upper World! The only way for me to get home is with this giant's help!"

Eric stopped breathing. *Home? In the Upper World? In my world?*

"What does that mean?" Neal asked.

Julie started trembling. "He's scaring me."

"Dig, my Ninns! Dig!" Sparr shouted. "Dig up the rest of him! Zor shall rise again!"

As the Ninns dug away at the huge stones, the sorcerer stormed away into the tomb's darkness.

Zzzzt. The mirror faded.

The front window of the sub bubbled furiously. The water seemed lighter. Max was steering the ship up through the water.

Up to the surface.

Galen nodded gravely. "Now our real journey begins. Our journey to find Lord Sparr. And to stop him!"

Julie peered through the window as the sub splashed above the surface. "There's land ahead. A long beach and big brown hills beyond."

Keeah nodded. "The shores of Panjibarrh. They call it the land of dust."

Neal gulped loudly. "Just so everybody knows," he said, "I'm allergic to dust."

Four

Welcome to Panjibarrh!

The submarine rumbled out onto the beach and stopped on the sand.

Pop! Everyone piled out of the top hatch.

Before them stretched a row of small hills. Behind that was a range of larger hills. Beyond that were even taller hills. As far as the eye could see, everything was dusty, brown, and smooth.

"Panjibarrh seems kind of boring," Neal said.

"Let us hope it stays boring," Max chirped. "But this is Droon. Anything can happen."

Galen turned to the ship, uttered a short command, and the ship rumbled back into the water.

Keeah scanned the hills. Then she took a deep breath and clutched her feather necklace.

"Lord Sparr is somewhere in these hills," she said. "I can feel him nearby. Let's find him."

For the next hour, the small band climbed through narrow passes that ran between the hillsides. From one range to another, the six travelers slowly wormed their way upward.

Entering one steep pass, Galen stopped.

He turned his head slowly. He narrowed his eyes.

"There . . ." he murmured. "That shadowy hole in the rocks. There is something in there."

Max began to quake. "What is it, master?"

Galen gazed deeply into the shadows. "A cave. And — *he* is there." He turned to Keeah.

"Princess," he said, "I sense something evil in there. If what I feel in my heart is true, Sparr's plan is even more terrible than we thought. I must go in. You and the others wait here."

"Be careful, master," Max chittered.

The wizard smiled at the spider troll. "My time has not yet come, my friend. Don't worry."

With that, Galen wrapped his robe around him and entered the cave alone.

Strange sounds echoed suddenly from the hills above. Low, rumbling sounds. Then the air went still. Silence fell over the pass.

"That's weird," Julie whispered. "It's like all the sound in the world just stopped."

Neal squinted up at the hills. "Do you think it's Lord Sparr —"

Whoosh!

A burst of wind swept up from the dusty ground. It spun faster and faster. It coiled around in the air, forming a dark, whirling funnel.

"Yikes!" said Eric, shielding his eyes. "Let's get out of here!"

But the wind struck quickly. As if it were alive, the coil of spinning dust leaped upon the five friends, scattering them.

"Take cover, everyone!" Keeah cried out, grabbing Max and pulling him to the shelter of an overhanging rock.

Julie tried to join them but stumbled on the rocky ground. She struggled to her feet, but the funnel tore after her, whirling and spitting dust.

"Help!" she cried, trying to outrun the wind.

Neal bolted from his hiding place. "Julie!"

Keeah, too, leaped from shelter to face the furious funnel. She clutched her feather and cried out, but her words were lost in the fury of the storm.

The wind swept around Julie, surrounding her. "It's got me!" she shrieked.

The wind pulled her inside itself.

Eric stumbled toward the funnel, his arms outstretched. "Julie! Here!" he shouted. The spinning dust stung his face. "I'm coming!" he cried.

But the wind wouldn't let him come.

The twister spun Julie around and

around. It roared up the side of the pass. Up and up it went, spinning Julie away with it, until her cries were lost.

"JULIE!" Eric shouted for the last time.

A moment later, the dark funnel was gone.

The wind in the pass died down to nothing.

The storm was over.

And Julie was gone.

Five

A Hidden Village

"The storm went that way!" Keeah said, pointing to the highest range of hills. "We have to find Julie. And we need to hurry. Come on!"

"What about Galen?" Neal asked.

"He is Droon's greatest wizard," said Max, already scampering up the hillside after Keeah. "Galen Longbeard can take care of himself!"

The four friends raced into the hills, following the track of the dust storm. Hill after hill they climbed. Higher and higher they went.

"What if we can't find her?" said Neal, breathing hard as he scrambled up a rocky hillside.

"No way!" Eric snapped. "Julie's special. We'll find her. We've got to keep going. We've got to."

Max spun a spider silk rope and swung from ledge to ledge, moving ahead of everyone.

Suddenly, he stopped and pointed his pug nose in the air. He sniffed. "Smoke," he said.

"Smoke usually means people," said Keeah.

Neal nodded. "Be careful. Careful is good."

They followed the smoky smell until they came to a break between the hills.

Clustered along one hillside were dozens of small houses. They had domed roofs made of dried mud.

Smoke wafted up from their chimneys.

"A village," Eric whispered.

In the exact center of the village was a large round platform.

It looked like a giant wheel lying on its side.

And in the exact center of the wheel was —

"Julie!" Keeah said.

Surrounding Julie were hundreds of small creatures covered in red fur. Each one was about three feet tall. They had doglike snouts covered with whiskers, except for small black noses at the tips. Their ears were pointy and very long.

"She's a prisoner," Neal said. "And we're outnumbered. Any ideas?"

"Perhaps a little magic will help," Keeah

said. She waved her hand over the four of them. The air turned a misty pink.

"The fog of invisibility!" Max chirped. "Galen taught you well, Princess. Come, let us enter."

Hidden by the pink fog, the four friends crept quietly into the village. No one saw them.

The largest of the strange, furry creatures stepped across the giant wheel to Julie.

"Now . . ." he said, curling and uncurling his nose whiskers, ". . . now, you will get it!"

Julie shook her head. "No . . . please . . ."

Eric stole a look at Neal and Keeah. "She's in trouble. We need to get her out of there — now!"

"Bring the black helmet!" the furry creature commanded. "I, Batamogi, King of the Oobja, shall put it right on her head!"

Eric couldn't stand it anymore. He jumped out of the pink fog and ran up to the platform.

"Stop!" he shouted at the top of his lungs. "Julie is our friend. You leave her alone!"

All the pointy-eared creatures turned. Julie blinked over their heads. "Eric?"

The small, furry king turned. "Who is *Eric*?"

"*I'm* Eric!" said Eric. "And if you hurt Julie, we'll be all over you like . . . like . . ."

Neal jumped out of the fog next to Eric. "Like cheese on a pizza!"

"So don't hurt her!" Keeah shouted, jumping out of the fog with Max.

Batamogi stumbled backward. "*Hurt* her? But . . . Julie is our new princess! She has come to help our people. We are going to *crown* her."

Eric frowned. "What? Oh, sure. Crown her. With something nasty called the *black helmet?*"

The fox-eared leader held up the shiny helmet.

It was covered with beautiful jewels.

"Black goes better with her hair," the king said. "We have a nice pink helmet and two powder-blue ones. But I think black is her color."

Eric blinked. "Oh . . . um . . . well . . ."

Julie laughed and jumped over to her friends. "These people aren't hurting me," she said. "The storm set me down in their village. They've been really, really nice! And it's just like my dream!"

She turned to the crowd. "Everybody, meet Eric, Neal, Keeah, and Max."

The furry king bowed nearly to the ground. "I am Batamogi, King of the Oobja. We are the mole people of the Pan-jibarrh hills."

Batamogi bowed again to Keeah. "Welcome, Princess. All of Droon knows you. But there is another princess here, too. Princess Julie."

He handed Julie the shiny black helmet encrusted with jewels.

Julie laughed. "I'm really just a regular kid."

The king tapped his furry head. "All mole people can sense things. We can tell when someone has powers even before they do. And believe me, Julie, you have powers. You will help us, you'll see."

Julie blinked as she slid the jeweled helmet on. "Cool," she said. "But I still don't believe it."

Keeah turned to the fox-eared, red-furred king. "We have come here to find Lord Sparr."

The mole people gasped and pulled back.

"Sparr!" Batamogi snorted with anger. "We do not like him. We are peaceful people. But Sparr demanded we show him where Zor's tomb is. We have known for ages that Zor lies in the ancient realm of Goll. It is right under these hills. When my brothers refused to tell Sparr, he took them away. He said that he would hurt them if I didn't show him where the giant was buried."

Batamogi sniffled and wiped his snout on his furry wrist. "I had to do what he asked!"

"That's why we're here," Eric said. "We need to stop Sparr from bringing Zor back to life."

The Oobja king sniffled once more, then stood up straight. "Then I will show you where Sparr and his Ninns are. Yes! But first, we feast. Come, my people. Click-clack!"

The Oobja people laughed softly to themselves and scurried away on their short legs. Moments later they were back, carrying a flat, round bread as big as the big wooden wheel itself.

"Flat bread baked with red sauce and cheese," Batamogi said. "We like them big. Sometimes we sit in the middle and eat our way to the crust!"

Neal's mouth dropped open. He stared at Eric. "Whoa! I guess I *did* dream of Droon last night. Only I didn't know it."

Eric smiled as he chewed. He wondered if he, too, had dreamed of Droon without knowing it.

"Eat up!" Batamogi urged. "Our mission is dangerous."

He ripped off a piece of cheesy bread and, bowing his head, handed it to Princess Julie.

"And Lord Sparr will do everything he can to stop us!"

Six

A New Enemy?

Batamogi led the children down from the big round platform. His people joined him.

"What is the big wheel, anyway?" Eric asked.

The Oobja king smoothed his whiskers. "Ah, yes, well, let me explain —"

"There's a big stick here," Neal said, peering around the wheel. "Like a control stick. What happens if you push it —"

Errrch! The stick squeaked as Neal touched it.

At once the wheel began to spin. Then a loud whooshing sound came from nowhere. A whirling storm of dust exploded up from the ground. It encircled Neal and swept him up in the air.

"Whoa!" he yelled. "Help me!"

Batamogi quickly pushed the stick back down.

The dust storm disappeared and — *plop!* — Neal landed in a heap on the ground.

Julie laughed. "That's how I got here!"

Batamogi helped Neal up and brushed him off. "We call this our Wind Wheel. We use it to make dust storms to keep others from finding our village. Too bad it didn't keep Sparr from stealing my brothers."

Then the king led the children to the

edge of the village. He turned and waved to his people.

They waved back from the big wheel.

"Where are your brothers?" Keeah asked.

The king tapped his forehead again. "I don't know. But something tells me they are alive."

Sunlight slanted across the dust hills as Batamogi led the troop into a narrow pass. The hills on either side rose hundreds of feet in the air.

The fox-eared king pointed up ahead. "Sparr brought his Ninns through this pass. They came to dig up the giant. We are not far now."

Eric shared a glance with his friends. They were heading straight for Lord Sparr.

"I know I say 'careful' a lot," Neal said. "But maybe now is a good time. You never know when something might —"

Fwap! Fwap! The sound of wings filled the air.

"Hrooooo!" came a loud cry.

"Groggles?" Neal yelped.

"No! Worse!" Batamogi replied. "Hide!"

The air grew hot, and a burst of blue flame shot across the hills above them. Then a giant blue wing flapped overhead. It was scaly and rough. A spiky arm clawed at the sky.

"A dragon!" Keeah whispered, touching her feather necklace. "It's all blue!"

Dust and rocks crumbled from the hillsides and into the pass in front of the kids. The shadow of the dragon's wing glided over them.

"Hrooooo!" The dragon's call coiled down once more. Then the shadow vanished.

Sunlight flooded the high walls again.

The dragon was gone.

Batamogi waddled to the middle of the pass and looked up. "This dragon has been here since Sparr arrived, frightening my people. The hills used to be quiet. I hope they will be quiet again."

Clank! Clong! From nearby came the sounds of metal and stone banging together.

"Digging?" Eric whispered.

The king nodded. "Come, we're nearly there."

Quietly, they tiptoed to the end of the passage. Beyond the last range of hills lay a small valley.

"Holy cow!" Julie said.

The valley lay torn open. Piles of sand-colored rocks were strewn about. Flying lizards called groggles whined loudly as they helped to pull large stones out of the ground.

Lord Sparr stood by while hundreds of

his red warrior Ninns dug away at the earth.

"They're digging up the whole tomb," Keeah said. "They've dug up the resting place of Zor."

"He won't be resting long," Max said. "Look!"

Two Ninns dragged a heavy box across the dirt. Eric and his friends recognized that box. It contained Zor's amulet. Sparr had stolen it when he turned Jaffa City to ice. With the amulet, Sparr could bring the dead giant back to life.

The Ninns opened the box. Sparr took out the large black amulet. The jewel in its center glistened in the sunlight. The sorcerer began to laugh.

"He's going to do it!" Neal whispered.

Sparr stepped down into the open tomb. Slowly, he strode across the giant's dark chest.

He set the amulet into a spot near Zor's neck.

Click! It fit perfectly into place.

The air grew hushed in the valley.

"Now what?" Eric whispered.

They heard a grunting noise behind them.

"Uh-oh," Neal mumbled.

The group turned around to find a fat, red-faced Ninn warrior standing over them.

"I've been expecting you!" he growled.

Seven

The Powers of Sparr

"That's it, we're doomed for sure!" Max chittered, scurrying behind his friends.

Then the Ninn smiled. And his fat red face began to change. It went pale, and a long white beard grew from his chin. His warrior's armor shriveled away and became a long blue robe.

"Galen!" Keeah said. "How did you get here?"

The wizard motioned them into the

shadows as he spoke. "The cave I saw was an old entrance to Goll. To avoid being captured, I pretended to be a Ninn. My friends, it's worse than we thought. Sparr wants to raise Zor for one reason only."

Keeah trembled. "What reason?"

"Ages ago, Zor came under the power of something called the Golden Wasp," Galen said. "Only the giant knows where it lies hidden."

"The Golden Wasp!" the princess exclaimed. "One of Sparr's Three Powers!"

Eric, Neal, and Julie shared a look.

They all remembered the first time Galen told them about Sparr's Three Powers. They were magical objects the sorcerer created so that he could take over Droon. When Galen found out, he put a spell over them to change their shape.

Now they were hidden; no one knew where.

The First Power was a jewel called the Red Eye of Dawn. It controlled the forces of nature.

"What does this Wasp thing do?" Neal asked.

"The Wasp is even more dangerous than the Eye of Dawn," Galen told them. "It controls the minds and thoughts of others."

Neal snorted. "Ha! It won't control *my* mind."

"Right," said Eric. "Only pizza does that. And ice cream. And peanut butter. Also nachos."

Neal frowned. "You're making me hungry."

Julie turned to Galen. "What can we do?"

But the wizard didn't answer. His eyes were filled with fear. "Look now!" he said.

Sparr stood over the giant's body. "By

the stars of Droon, rise, O ancient Zor! Rise!"

The ground began to rumble and quake.

Then, all at once, the giant's huge arms burst up from the ground, sending rocks flying everywhere. His legs kicked suddenly, shattering the earth. Then Zor lifted himself out of his tomb.

He struggled to his feet.

His tremendous shadow fell over the valley.

"Uh-oh," said Julie. "We have a problem."

"A big problem," Max chirped.

The dark eyes of the giant stared at the sorcerer beneath him. A simple lift of his foot would crush Lord Sparr in an instant.

But Zor did not crush him. He knelt before Sparr and bowed his head to him.

"Master!" the giant boomed. "What would you have me do?"

"Holy cow!" Eric whispered. "How are we going to stop that thing?"

"We can't!" Max chittered. "We're doomed!"

Sparr's face twisted into an evil grin. "Zor, I command you to find the Golden Wasp!"

Zor turned his head and stared at the sun. His dark eyes took on a fiery glow.

"With the Wasp, I, Lord Sparr, shall conquer all of Droon!" the sorcerer shouted. "Then I shall rise to the Upper World and conquer it, too!"

The Upper World! Eric thought. *My world.*

Sparr thrust his hand into the air. "Go, my giant! Find the Wasp!"

The giant swiveled his enormous body.

Thoom! He took a step.

Thoom! Another step.

"Go!" Sparr cried out. "Let nothing stop you!"

Eric couldn't take any more. He jumped out of the shadows and shook his fist at Zor.

"Nothing but us!" he cried. "We'll stop you!"

Thooom . . . The giant stopped. He turned his enormous bronze face.

He lowered his eyes at Eric and his friends.

"Um," Eric mumbled. "Did I really say that?"

"I think you did," Neal answered.

Sparr whirled around and pointed toward the children. "Zor! Destroy them!"

"Watch out, here he comes!" Batamogi yelled.

An enormous foot slammed to earth near the kids. *Thoom!*

Sparr began to laugh wildly. "Yes! Yes! Destroy them, once and for all!"

The giant's other foot lifted up over the kids.

Its huge shadow fell over them.

"Run!" cried Batamogi at the top of his lungs.

Eight

The Bronze Giant

Keeah leaped over and pushed Eric out of the way just in time.

Thoom! Zor's other foot slammed down. Then he stretched his giant arms toward Keeah.

"No!" Keeah slid down the hill toward Zor.

Suddenly, another cry filled the air. It echoed down from the hills above. "Hrooooo!"

"The blue dragon!" Neal shouted.

The dragon swooped toward Zor, but the giant was swift. He pulled a huge ledge off the side of the hill, broke it in half, and heaved the chunks of rock at the dragon.

"Begone, you beast!" Zor boomed.

The dragon clawed at him, crying out noisily. "Hrooooo — ooo!" Then it swooped down and clamped its jaws tightly on the giant's shoulder.

"ARRGH!" Zor howled, flailing his arms and losing his balance.

Wham! He fell back against the hills, sending a pile of rocks crashing into the valley below.

Eric leaped out of the way, tumbling to the ground next to Neal.

"Did you say something about Pan-jibarrh being boring?" Eric asked.

"Not me!" Neal said, scrambling away

just before Zor's huge foot slammed down near him.

Sparr's laughter turned to shouting. "Galen, you have bothered me once too often. Prepare to meet your doom!"

His fingertips sizzled with red flame.

The wizard scoffed. "You haven't seen the last of me, Sparr." He sent a bolt of blue light shooting across the valley at the sorcerer.

Ka-boom! It exploded at Sparr's feet, knocking him into the dust.

"It's two against one, Sparr!" Keeah cried. She followed the wizard's bolt with one of her own.

Ka-boom-oom! Sparr fell once again.

Together, the two wizards pushed Sparr deep into the remains of Zor's dark tomb. They followed him down into it, their blue light flashing up from the depths.

The dragon kept up its fierce attack on Zor.

"Arrgh!" the giant bellowed. He swatted the dragon. When it pulled back, he tried to stomp Neal and Julie, but they scurried out of the way.

"Can't catch us!" Julie yelled. "We're special!"

"Hrooooo!" The dragon circled the giant. It opened its jaws wide and breathed a blast of fiery blue flame. Zor shielded his face and stomped away from the children.

Another blast of blue fire sent Zor reeling back even farther.

"The dragon is winning!" Eric shouted.

Then the sky above the valley burned red.

Sparr flew up from the depths of the tomb to a high rock. He shot bolt after bolt of red light back down into the tomb.

And from the tomb's darkness came a scream.

"It's Keeah!" Max cried. "She's in trouble!"

The dragon turned in midflight. Its deep green eyes pierced the dusty air. "Hrooooo!"

Eric stared at the large blue beast. Its eyes showed — what? Fear. And something else, too.

"The dragon needs to help Keeah!" Eric called out. "Come on, guys. Let's keep Zor busy!"

Neal and Julie heaved rocks at the giant. Eric grabbed a Ninn shovel and began whacking Zor's huge feet. *Bing! Bang! Bong!*

"Hey!" Neal shouted. "Your dream, Eric. Hitting a garbage can. That's just what Zor is!"

Eric laughed as he kept on banging. "I *did* dream of Droon after all! Hey, I'm special, too!"

While the dragon flew at Sparr, the sorcerer began uttering strange ancient words.

"*Zor — katoo — selam — teeka — meth!*"

A red cloud swirled up from Sparr and shot across to Zor. The cloud was sucked into the amulet. The amulet's crystal glowed red-hot.

"RRRR!" the giant roared. "Destroy the village! Destroy the village!"

Zor heaved his arms high in the air. He turned to the dust hills and began to climb.

"No!" Batamogi cried. "Oh, my poor people!"

Thomp! Thomp! The earth quaked with each step. A thick cloud of dust poured over the kids.

Eric shielded his eyes, but the dust

stung him. "I can't see anything," he said, stumbling.

Julie rushed to him. "Rub your eyes, Eric."

He balled up his fists and rubbed his eyes to clear them. "Thanks. Now let's get out of here."

Julie stared at Eric. She gasped. She whirled to her feet. "That's it! Come on, everybody! We can stop this nasty metal-brained giant."

"How?" Neal asked, running after her.

"With what these hills are famous for," said Julie. "Dust!"

Nine

Dust Is Our Friend

Thomp! Thomp! The giant clomped up the hills toward the Oobja village.

Batamogi waddled as fast as his short legs could carry him. His whiskers curled in fear. "I hope we can save my people!"

Julie raced next to him, her black helmet shining in the afternoon sun. "We'll save them. Don't worry."

Wham! Bam! Zor hurled boulders at the kids.

"Well, okay. Worry a little!" Julie said, pulling the king out of the way just as a boulder crashed nearby.

They dashed through the pass and into the village before Zor got there.

The Oobja were hiding in their homes.

The kids rushed to the big wooden wheel.

Batamogi ran to the control stick. "Princess Julie, the honor is yours!"

Julie nodded, then pulled the control stick as Neal had done before. *Errrch!* The Wind Wheel began to turn. It spun faster and faster.

Whooosh! A dark funnel of dust started up from the middle of the wheel. It rose high into the sky, spinning like a tornado.

"I'm good at controlling things," Max chirped. "Let me help." He wrapped his eight legs around the control stick and pulled hard.

King Batamogi joined him.

Whooosh! The dust funnel shot up the hillside.

Then, there he was.

Zor. His giant bronze head peered between two peaks. He hoisted himself up and climbed through. "ARRR!" he bellowed down at them.

Just as he lifted his giant foot to stomp the village, the dust storm spun up at him.

Zor raised his giant arms in front of his face. He backed away, pawing at the spinning wind.

"He can't see," Eric said. "It's working!"

Zor backed up to the summit of the highest hill. He shielded his eyes with one hand and swatted the brown spinning air with the other.

Still the dust storm came at him.

Zor stepped backward once more.

Krrrakk! The ledge beneath him gave way.

"AHHH!" the giant screamed.

He tumbled backward off the mountain and hit the valley below with a thundering crash. *BOO-OOM!*

Batamogi and Max slowed the wheel. The dust storm died away. The village fell quiet.

The kids rushed down to the giant metal man. His bronze body was cracked and crumpled.

He shuddered, then lay still.

His giant lips quivered.

"Shh, everyone," Eric said, creeping slowly closer. "Zor's going to say something."

"A . . . A . . . Agrah-Voor!" the giant said. He breathed a single long breath.

Then he spoke no more.

He trembled once, and his dark eyes closed.

"What's Agrah-Voor?" Neal asked.

KKKK! The sky turned red above them.

"Never mind that! Sparr is coming!" said Julie.

A second later, Sparr shot down from the sky. He landed on the dusty plain next to Zor.

His face was filled with anger.

His purple fins turned black.

"He doesn't look happy," Neal muttered.

The spiky points running back from the middle of Sparr's head seemed to glow bloodred.

"Ah, my Zor, my Zor! Giant man of bronze," Sparr said. "For ages you have lain asleep, waiting to do my will! And now . . ."

"Yeah, sorry he's all broken up," Eric said.

"Bring the garbage truck," Neal added.

Sparr turned. "You puny children think you have beaten me? This is just the beginning. You will never win. Now tell me what Zor said!"

Eric made a zipper motion across his mouth.

Julie shook her head and crossed her arms.

"Tell me!" Sparr commanded. "Or else."

Finally, Neal raised his hand. "Zor said . . ."

"What?" the sorcerer shrieked.

Neal frowned. "He said you should . . ."

"Yes?" the sorcerer said.

"He said you should get a life!" Neal finished.

Sparr rose up over Neal. His eyes flashed with terrible anger. "Those were your last words, you foolish child. Now, all of you, prepare to meet your doom!"

Eric gulped and turned to Neal and Julie. "Doom. That's not really a good thing, is it?"

Neal shook his head. "I'm pretty sure it's not."

Ten

One Last Thing?

Kla-blam! A bolt of blue light shot across the hills and exploded next to Sparr.

The kids turned. "Hooray!" they cheered.

Through the dust strode Galen and Keeah. Their hands were raised at Sparr. Their fingertips sizzled with blue sparks.

"Begone, Sparr!" Galen said. "You have lost!"

Eric grinned. "This just isn't your day, Sparr."

"Hrooooo!" The dragon swooped overhead.

And from the village came hundreds of Oobjas. They marched at Sparr, looking angry.

The sorcerer growled like a captive animal.

He raised his arms to the sky, flapped his cloak like a set of wings, and shot up into the air.

"Come, my Ninns," he called out bitterly. "We live to fight another day! Victory will be ours!"

Instantly, his red-faced warrior Ninns took to their groggles. The sky darkened over the dust hills as they swarmed after their leader.

Moments later, Sparr and his army were gone.

"Yahoo! We beat him!" Neal shouted, jumping up and down. "We won today! We won!"

"Excellent work, my friends," Galen said.

The giant lay motionless before them, his dark eyes crusted with dust.

"Your plan worked," Keeah said to Julie.

The Oobja king smiled broadly. "I told you she had powers. The powers of imagination!"

Julie smiled. "Well, the dragon sure helped."

Princess Keeah looked up. The dragon was perched quietly on a hill overlooking the village.

Its deep green eyes met Keeah's. An unspoken word seemed to pass between them.

Then Keeah gasped. "Oh, my gosh! Mother?"

"Hrooooo!" the dragon cried.

"I knew it!" Max chirped. "It is Queen Relna! That's why she helped us so much. My princess, the dragon is your mother!"

Keeah ran over as the blue dragon fluttered down and landed softly at the edge of the village. Keeah seemed to understand the soft, deep sounds her mother was making.

"A dragon queen," said Neal. "That is so awesome."

Galen smiled. "They are together once again."

"Families should be together," said Max.

Batamogi sniffled once. "I wish my nine brothers were here to see this day."

Julie looked at the furry king. "Wait.

Did you say *nine* brothers? You have *nine* brothers?"

Batamogi nodded. "We ruled our village together. We were all crowned at birth."

Julie blinked. "Nine brothers, nine kings, nine . . . *crowns*?"

Eric gasped at Julie. "Your dream!"

"My dream!" Julie repeated. "I was floating over a hilltop and saw nine crowns . . . oh, my gosh! I understand it now. I understand it!"

Julie ran over to Keeah and her mother. "Can your mother take us someplace?"

The dragon murmured to Keeah.

Keeah laughed. "She'd be delighted!"

Julie jumped. "Come on, everyone. King Batamogi, get ready for a family reunion!"

Everyone piled onto Queen Relna's back. Julie pointed over the hills. The queen flapped her long wings once and lifted off the ground.

"This is just like my dream," Julie said. "I was floating high over Droon."

"And you wore a crown," Neal said, tapping Julie's black helmet. "Just like you are now."

The dragon dipped over the green lake and came to rest on the hilltop where Eric, Julie, and Neal had begun their journey.

On top of the hill was the circle of nine strange trees. They stood like statues in the fading sunlight. Their tangled branches reached to the sky.

Julie turned to Batamogi. "In my dream," she said, "there were nine crowns sitting on a hilltop. Here there are nine trees. When your brothers refused to help Sparr, he must have enchanted them. He changed them. Into trees!"

"When they grabbed us, they weren't

trying to hurt us," Neal said. "They wanted us to help them!"

"There is a spell to free them," Galen said. "And Keeah, you must help me."

The two wizards joined hands. Together, they began to murmur, *"Teppi — qualem — bratoo!"*

A blue mist wrapped around the trees.

The branches twitched and creaked.

The trees shrank to the size of bushes, and their leaves bunched up and became red fur. Their thick roots became squat legs. Their upper limbs became arms. Then, the circle of trees quivered together and became Batamogi's nine brothers.

"Oh, my! Oh, my!" Batamogi cried. "You see, Julie, you did help us. Now we do the dance of joy!"

The ten squat kings hugged one another. They linked arms and twirled around, laughing.

As they did, Eric turned to Galen. "Zor said one last thing before he went quiet. He said . . . Agrah-Voor."

Galen's eyes went wide. "Agrah-Voor is the legendary Land of the Lost. It is peopled by the heroes of Droon's past."

Max shivered. "They say that the only way to enter Agrah-Voor is to be a . . . a . . . ghost!"

Neal backed away. "So I guess we're not going there." He looked around. No one said a word.

"Tell me we are *not* going there!" he said.

Keeah smiled a big smile. "I think you already know the answer to that one, Neal."

He frowned. Then he shrugged. Then he smiled. "Agrah-Voor, huh? Where the ghost people live? I know what I'll dream about tonight!"

Whoosh! A cool wind blew across the dust hills. The children looked up. Hovering over a rocky ledge nearby was the magic stairway.

"It looks like our adventure is over for today," Julie said, removing her helmet. "Time to go."

Batamogi took the helmet. "We'll keep this in a place of honor, Princess. For when you return."

"I hope I do return," Julie said.

Batamogi chuckled softly and tapped his head. "Sparr was right about one thing. This is just the beginning. You'll be back. I know you will."

The three friends stepped onto the stairs.

Keeah waved to them. "Keep the magic alive!"

"You bet we will!" Eric called back.

Then the princess, the wizard, the spider troll, and the ten kings of Panjibarrh all climbed onto Queen Relna's back. The dragon circled the stairs once and headed toward the sun.

Eric, Julie, and Neal waved good-bye and started up the stairs.

Then Eric stopped.

"Wait," he said. "Why didn't the stairs work for me or Neal? I mean, it turned out that we all dreamed of Droon. But they only worked for Julie."

Neal scratched his head. "What if the stairs worked because all three of us were there?"

"That's it," said Julie. "To make the stairs work we all have to go together. Because no one is more special than anybody else. That's cool."

Neal nodded. "It's like we dreamed three parts of the same dream."

Eric thought about that for a while.

Then he smiled. "Three parts of the same dream. Cool. I can live with that."

"Me, too," Neal said. "I mean, we're a team, right?"

Julie grinned. "The absolute best."

She put up her hand.

Eric and Neal slapped her high fives. She did the same back to them.

The three friends took one more look at the land of Droon, then raced up the stairs for home.

ABOUT THE AUTHOR

Tony Abbott is the author of more than two dozen funny novels for young readers, including the popular *Danger Guys* books and *The Weird Zone* series. Since childhood he has been drawn to stories that challenge the imagination, and, like Eric, Julie, and Neal, he often dreamed of finding doors that open to other worlds. Now that he is older — though not quite as old as Galen Longbeard — he believes he may have found some of those doors. They are called books. Tony Abbott was born in Ohio and now lives with his wife and two daughters in Connecticut.

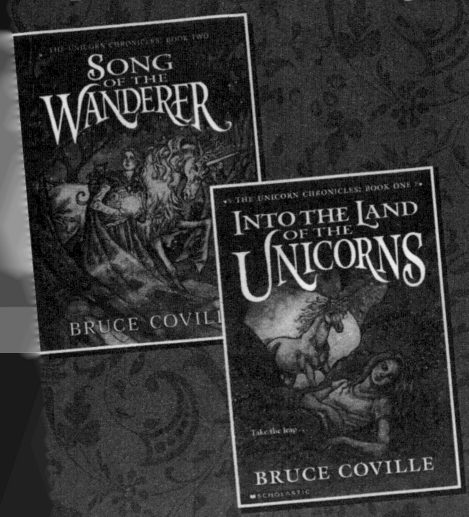